A Boy
Like That

Tony Langham
Illustrated by Tracy Fennell

A & C Black · London

GRAFFIX

Roller Madonnas · Bernard Ashley
Roy Kane TV Detective · Steve Bowkett
Bodyparts · Theresa Breslin
Moving the Goalposts · Rob Childs
Captain Hawk · Jim Eldridge
Laser Quest · Mick Gowar
Matthew's Goals · Michael Hardcastle
Thirteen Candles · Mary Hooper
The Headless Ghost · Pete Johnson
The Listener · Elizabeth Laird
A Boy Like That · Tony Langham
Biker · Anthony Masters
Otherworld · Jeremy Strong
Lovesick · Lynda Waterhouse

First paperback edition 1999
First published 1998 in hardback by
A & C Black (Publishers) Ltd
35 Bedford Row, London WC1R 4JH

ISBN 0-7136-4988-7

A CIP catalogue for this book is available from
the British Library.

Printed and bound in Spain by G. Z. Printek, Bilbao.

Chapter One

It was the first day back at school after the summer break. I was really glad to be back - back with my two best friends, Chrissy and Gita.

Hi, Beth! You look great! Fabulous tan!

Did you have a good time? What are Greek boys like? We want to hear all about it.

I'd been to Greece with my parents. You'd think that would've been wonderful, wouldn't you? Wonderful scenery, warm sea, handsome Greek boys...

Dad smiled and shook his head. He didn't really approve of Chrissy and Gita. He thought they were both a bit too crazy, which was true. It's about the only thing we agreed on. Gita steered me away from the car.

Sorry, Mr Clarke, but we've got to go. We don't want to be late on our first day back.

As soon as we were out of earshot, Chrissy began the questions.

I don't believe you. You're telling us, Bethany Clarke, that you went all the way to Greece and didn't meet one Greek hunk?

The expressions on their faces were priceless. They both looked really miserable. I couldn't let the opportunity go to waste.

Unless you want to count Spiro, our waiter in the hotel.

9

Chrissy and Gita perked up at the mention of Spiro's name. Chrissy caught hold of my arm and stopped me in my tracks.
Spit it out - he was gorgeous wasn't he?
A god.

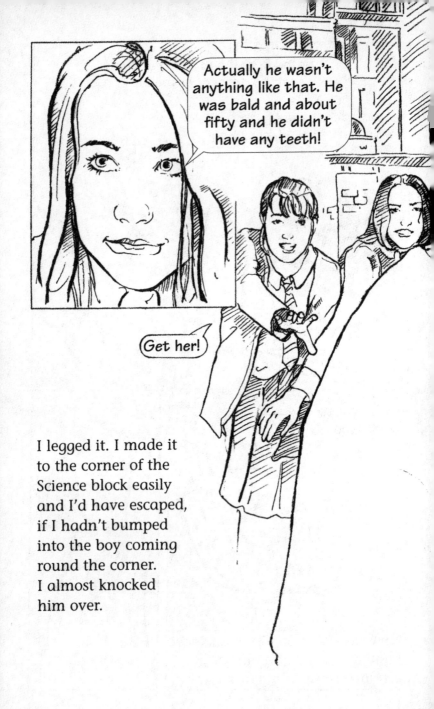

Actually he wasn't anything like that. He was bald and about fifty and he didn't have any teeth!

Get her!

I legged it. I made it to the corner of the Science block easily and I'd have escaped, if I hadn't bumped into the boy coming round the corner. I almost knocked him over.

15

He was still holding me when Chrissy and Gita turned the corner. They skidded to a halt like a couple of cartoon characters when they saw us, and their eyes popped out of their sockets when they saw him.

He was a head taller than me. His hair was dark and quite long, but the best thing about him was his eyes. They were incredible! A deep greenish-blue. I couldn't stop looking into them. It was like being hypnotised.

You're a bit old to play tig, aren't you?

I was... I mean... we were...

Playing tig, like you said.

Want to join in?

Trust Gita to get right to the point.

He gave me a parting smile that made me go weak at the knees.

We all watched him walk across the yard to the main building. He even had a cool walk - I couldn't take my eyes off him.

Gita nudged Chrissy and nodded in my direction.

19

Gita came up to me and put her head close.

I looked at Chrissy and Gita.
Chrissy laughed.

Chapter Two

There are nearly 1800 pupils at Beechgrove Comprehensive. It's a huge place. People have been known to disappear, never to be seen again, so I didn't know if I'd ever see him again. After all he could've just been a visitor to the school...

Could've been.

Yeah, could've been.

We were in the dining-room the second day back, and all we could talk about was him.

But he was wearing school uniform, wasn't he?

I shrugged. The only thing I could clearly remember were his eyes.

22

23

That wasn't true of course. Chrissy and Gita could read me like a book. To tell the truth I couldn't stop thinking about him. It was like being haunted.

And then on Friday we bumped into each other again. At least he bumped into me this time. I was in the library trying to catch up on some homework when someone walked past my table, knocking into it.

Sorry.

I looked up and there he was. My heart started beating like a drum.

We'll have to stop meeting like this.

Now if it had been Gita or Chrissy, they would have said something smart in reply, but I just sat there speechless, my mouth open. My tongue seemed to be stuck to the roof of my mouth.

He hesitated for a few seconds, then turned away and headed for the exit. Somehow I got out of my seat and went after him. As I reached the door, I ran into Chrissy and Gita.

Whoa, girl!

It's him... he was just here...

25

We dashed off down the corridor and caught up with him on the second floor. Peeking around a corner, we saw him talking to another boy.

That's Benny Parkes. We're in luck.

Why?

'Cos the fool's crazy about our Gita, here.

Is he?

Cool it. He's going.

We watched him leave. Benny Parkes started to walk off in the opposite direction.

Go get him, Gita!

Gita flicked back a frond of jet-black hair which had fallen over her eyes. She looked at me.

Watch and learn. And remember - you owe me.

Chrissy and I watched as Gita approached her victim. It only took her a couple of minutes to get the information we needed. Benny Parkes didn't stand a chance. Gita came back, smiling broadly.

Well?

His name's Sanderson - get this, Rafe Sanderson.

Cool name.

He's just transferred from Breeze Hill Comp. He's a Year 8.

That made him a year older than me. Gita smiled. I swear she was reading my mind.

So all we've got to do is make sure you two lovebirds bump into each other again. Shouldn't be too difficult.

Piece of cake.

Chapter Three

There he is.

Once Gita and Chrissy decide to do something, they don't give up until they get it done. That's how I found myself in Ms Crane's drama group. They'd found out that Rafe was in it and had dragged me along to the gym.

We were at the door, peering through the window. I was getting cold feet.

Go for it!

They pushed me through the door.

Ms Crane was really pleased to have another member for her group.

I want you to enjoy yourself. You probably know some of the others, but I'll introduce you anyway. Take your shoes off.

I followed her back to the waiting group. Ms Crane clapped her hands to gain their attention.

Everybody, we have a new member - Bethany Clarke. I know you'll make her welcome. Right let's get on. Find a space...

I tried not to look at Rafe as we spread out. I really tried. But when I finally stole a quick glance at him, I almost collapsed. He smiled at me! It made my knees feel wobbly. We started out with some simple improvisations and followed up with some voice exercises. It turned out to be quite fun. When the session ended Rafe came across to me.

You going for lunch?

Sorry?

I'd heard him perfectly well enough. I was having trouble getting one of my shoes on.

Try the other foot.

I looked down and wanted the floor to swallow me up. I was trying to get my left shoe on to my right foot. I slipped the shoe off and smiled weakly at him.

Lunch. I wondered if you fancied going to lunch with me?

I managed to get my act together. I smoothed my hair out of my eyes and put my shoes on the right feet.

Let's go!

Sure.

We had a lovely lunch. Rafe was really easy to talk to and he was a good listener too, unlike most of the boys I knew. And to cap it all he made me laugh.

So what do you think of Beechgrove?

It's early days but it seems all right.

So how come you chose us?

I tried not to sound too grateful that he had. He gave me another devastating smile.

It came highly recommended.

Before I could ask him what he meant by that he suddenly looked at his watch.

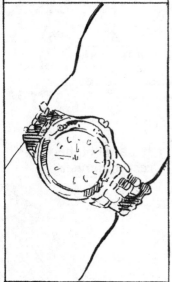

I managed not to add 'please' as he loped off.

They shrieked like a couple of apprentice witches.

It's karma!
Trust me, Beth.
I know these things.

She does, gets it
from her mum.

But by that time, I'd stopped listening. I was too busy running the 'Beth Clarke Meets Mr Right' video in my head.

Chapter Four

I was still on cloud nine at the end of the day. Dad gave me a strange look as we got into the car.

You look pleased with yourself.

Had a nice day.

That's good.

Dad coughed one of his coughs. He's got lots of different coughs. The one he'd just coughed was his 'I've-got-something-quite-serious-to-discuss-with-you' cough.

Just then the lights changed and Dad said he didn't want to discuss it any further in the car. Nor did he want to discuss things when we got home either. He just wouldn't tell me what he meant by 'a boy like that'.

I ran upstairs to my bedroom and threw myself down on my bed and cried and cried. Well, wouldn't you have done the same? I'd met someone very special and now I was being told I couldn't see him again! It wasn't fair!

I didn't sleep all night. I knew there was no point in asking Dad to change his mind. I needed some advice and I knew where to get it. As soon as I got to school the following day I told Gita and Chrissy what Dad had said. Chrissy shook her head.

The course of true love never runs smooth, does it Gita?

That's what they say.

But what am I going to do?

I hesitated for a few moments. I'd never gone against Dad's wishes before. But he wasn't being fair. He hadn't given Rafe a chance. He deserved a chance. Everybody does.

Chapter Five

The next morning I waited for Rafe to come out of assembly and asked him to meet me in the Library at morning break.

Gita and Chrissy came to the library with me and kept a look out in the corridor in case Dad happened along. Rafe was waiting for me.

So, what's the problem?

I told him. He didn't say anything until I finished, then he reached out and took my hands in his.

There was some trouble at Breeze Hill. And I was involved in it.

What kind of trouble?

My heart was beating madly. Rafe took a deep breath and explained.

A mate of mine was being bullied and I decided to help him out.

But things went a bit wrong and one of the kids who'd been doing the bullying ended up with a broken nose and I ended up in court.

And?

50

I'm sure we can work something out. We'll just have to ignore each other while we're in school.

That's going to be a little hard to do.

I could feel myself starting to blush. No boy had ever said anything like that to me before.

Gita and Chrissy hurried in after Rafe left. I told them
why he'd had to leave Breeze Hill Comprehensive.

'What about...' Chrissy began, but before she could make her suggestion the librarian came over to us and told us we'd have to leave because we were making too much noise.

Chapter Six

So Rafe and I ignored each other totally while we were at school. It drove me crazy not even being able to talk to him. Only Gita and Chrissy were in on our secret. They acted as go-betweens and set up all our meetings. And more. Like the time Gita asked my dad if I could go round to her house to work on a Geography project.

Ten was when I'd arranged to meet Rafe.

I climbed into the car. Dad started up the engine, but before he drove off he turned to me and said,

It's nice to see you setting a good example, Beth. I'm proud of you.

I felt bad about that. I'd never deceived my parents before, but my need to be with Rafe was so strong I was prepared to go to any lengths. I felt guilty about it, but there was no other way. Everything went fine for the first two weeks. Rafe and I met five times.

We're like a couple of spies.

James Bond and friend.

You don't look a bit like James Bond.

We had lots of fun. I was really happy - but I should have known it couldn't last. One Saturday afternoon, we pushed our luck a bit too far. I was supposed to be at Gita's working on our project, but I'd met Rafe in town. We were on our way to a café when we bumped into my mother. Mum was very pleasant, too pleasant.

Aren't you going to introduce me to your friend, Beth?

I introduced Rafe to her and she was very polite to him. Then she turned to me.

No way.
I'll come with you.

No.
I don't think that'd
be wise.

He hesitated, but I told him I'd be all right.
So Rafe went and I turned back to Mum.
She gave me one of her searching looks.

So who's going to tell
your father, me or you?

Me.

I wanted a chance to explain why I had done what I had although I knew that it wouldn't do any good. Dad took it very calmly. I apologised for lying to him and to Mum and tried to explain. Dad listened quietly, expressionless. But I could tell I hadn't convinced him.

You're wrong about Rafe. He's kind and considerate and understanding. He got into trouble trying to help a friend.

I nodded. It's difficult to explain how I felt.
Think of the worst moment you've ever
had and multiply that a hundred
times and you might be close.
I felt as if something had been
ripped out of me. I cried all
night and most of the next
day too. By Monday I'd just
about cried myself dry
and I went into school
dreading what I
had to do.

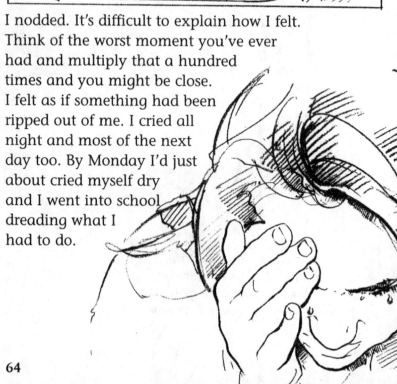

Chapter Seven

There's a small overgrown park next to the school. Nobody uses it much. It was just the place to meet Rafe and tell him I couldn't see him again. We arranged to meet at lunchtime. He was waiting for me when I arrived.

Are you all right?

Let's sit down.

65

We walked to the nearest bench and sat down. Rafe put his arm around me and pulled me close. I put my head on his shoulder. It felt so perfect, but I knew it was the last time I'd be doing it and I felt the tears welling up in my eyes. I took a deep breath and forced them back. There was no point putting it off any longer.

I can't see you again.

Rafe put a hand under my chin and forced me to look at him. He looked so sad and wounded.

Don't say that.

I'll go and see your dad and tell him how I feel... how we feel.
He won't listen. Once he's made up his mind he never changes it. You'll only cause more trouble for yourself. I don't want that.
We can't just let go of each other.

He stood up with his back to me, his head raised as if searching the sky for an answer. I got up, put my arms around him and held him close, burying my face in his back.
We stood like that for a few moments and then Rafe turned in my arms and looked down into my face. He'd been crying. The tracks of his tears glistened on his cheeks.

But he **doesn't** know that I love you.

His voice sounded so sad. Now I couldn't hold back my tears and I started to cry too. We probably only stood there a few moments, but it felt like an infinity.

Then I felt his arms go slack and he gently held me at arms length, then he kissed me for one last time. I watched him walk away.

At the park gates he stopped and turned. For a moment I thought he was going to come running back, but he didn't. I stepped back and sat down on the bench. I felt sick and dizzy. My head fell back, I closed my eyes and I took a deep breath.

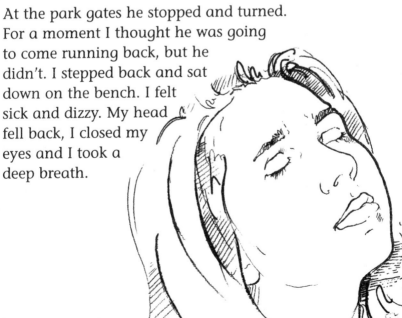

That was when I heard the squeal of brakes on the road outside the park. I heard a woman scream and then the sound of running feet. I got up and started running. Somehow I knew it all had something to do with Rafe. I saw the crowd as I ran through the gates. I pushed my way through the people.

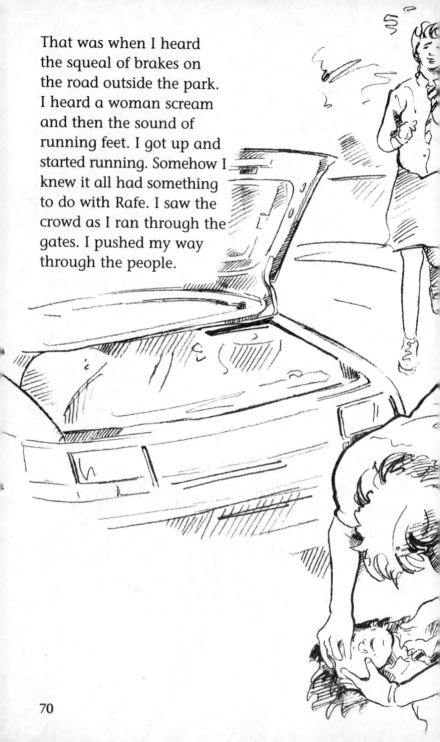

Rafe was lying on the road. His eyes were closed and there was blood coming from his head and trickling out of his mouth.

Rafe!

I screamed and then everything went dark...

71

The next thing I remember
was Dad asking me if
I was feeling better.

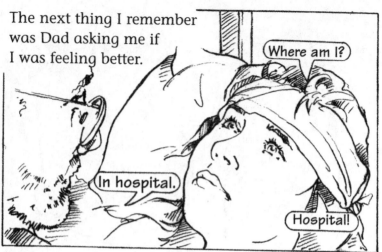

I sat up quickly and then wished I hadn't.
My head throbbed with pain.

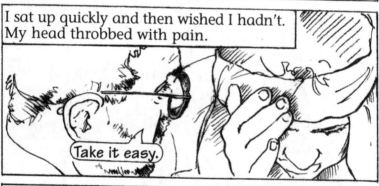

Then suddenly I remembered
Rafe. I saw everything again
in vivid detail! I tried to stand
up and almost collapsed.

A nurse came in. She made me lie down again and gave me a tablet.

It'll help the pain. You took a nasty knock on your head.

I felt my head with my hand. I was wearing a bandage.

You fainted when you saw Rafe. And banged your head.

They brought you in with Rafe.

But I had to wait. Rafe regained consciousness three days later and everybody wanted to see him and talk to the young hero who had saved a child from falling under the wheels of a lorry. Even the Mayor visited Rafe.

It was Dad who finally arranged my visit. You could say that he'd changed his mind about Rafe. He drove me to the hospital. Gita and Chrissy came along for the ride.

Gita and Chrissy stayed outside the room. Rafe was asleep when I went in. His head was bandaged and his face was badly bruised. He looked so fragile I almost burst out crying. I tiptoed to his bed and sat down. Reaching out I touched his fingers as gently as I could. But not gently enough. His eyes flickered open.

I leaned over and kissed him.

But I was too happy to think any more. I bent my head and kissed him again.